G000229456

Our

Humphrey

<u>Dedications</u>

First and foremost, to my great granduncle who perished in World War One. To all of those brave soldiers who fought, side by side, in the British Army for what they saw as a great adventure for king and country. Such a tragic loss.

To my dad who discovered the soldier you are going to read about. He too is an old soldier who has seen his share of conflict and I hope he has found his peace. This story will hit home.....

The soldier was stood there, alone in this world,
Alert and aware, like he should.
A shot rang out and he fell to the ground,
And he gasped at the sight of his blood.

His friends were around him, crying like mothers,
Watching this youthful life die,
He looked up from the ground, where he lay,
As he uttered his one last goodbye.

His friends were gone now, lost in his mind,
As he thought of his girl back at home,
"I'm sorry my love, for I must leave,
And this place, my spirit to roam."

He felt like he was drifting and he whispered his panic,
People started to gather in the street,
His body was gradually coming to a close,
As death, this time, he would not cheat.

Why was he there? Did he have to die?
Why was he in this tortured place?
Everyone hoped that whoever pulled the trigger,
Would remember his terrified face.

Before he came here, he'd written some words,
A few verses to remember him by.
They were read at the burial of this poor boy,
And nobody could do anything but cry.

"Like the rising of the sun on a birth of a day,
Like the clouds that glide slowly in the sky,
Like the wind that whistles through the trees,
There must come a time to die.

So think of me then, don't think of me now,
And think of the times that we had,
And think of the wonderful things that we did,
But please, I beg you, don't be sad.

My spirit is with you, wherever you go,
You may hear me whisper in your ear,
It may be the wind, or the swooping of birds,
But somehow you'll know that I'm near.

Shed no tears then at the place of my rest,
My life has been good and so fine,
Remember I'm with you as you walk this great land,
As I say goodbye for the last time."

Chapters

<u>Prologue</u>

I don't think anyone reading this book is going to believe what happened to me as a boy of ten years old. Some of you who believe in the afterlife might do, most of you won't. It doesn't matter; I know.

Dad had been tracing the Hirst family tree and came across my great granduncle, Humphrey Hirst, who served in the King's Own Yorkshire Light Infantry and informed me of his findings sometime in the year 2010. He made an internet search and found his burial plot in a military cemetery in France and so we planned to go over and visit him on our motorbikes to pay our respects.

What dad doesn't know, or anyone else come to think of it and what I had kept for all this time as a secret, is that I had already met Humphrey.

This is his story.

Chapter One: Me, 10 years old

Dad was in the British Army and rose to the rank of Sergeant in the Royal Military Police and served for fourteen years, returning to civilian life (Civvy Street they call it) in 1980 when I was eleven years old.

His last posting was Bovington Camp in Dorset, famous for its tank museum. He was going to spend the last two years of his service training the Junior Leaders, which was an avenue for sixteen year olds to join the Army before moving on to the adult British Army.

My brother, Steven and I attended our new school; the Bovington Middle School (which still exists the last time I looked).

I have few memories of that time, but they are still very vivid and at the end of one week at school, our teacher informed the class we were to learn about World War One the following week.

We all looked at one another, the boys showed excitement on their faces, the girls were not happy but stayed quiet. This was school after all and you did what you were told.

We lived in married quarters in Bovington, along a row of houses on a street called Andover Green. Steven and I had separate bedrooms and we had a good bunch of friends whose fathers were in different regiments. This fact didn't taint any friendship between us all, with no regimental rivalry and we led a happy life. My bedroom was at the front of the house, overlooking Andover Green and at night, the streetlight shadows from a tree outside swaying with the wind, cast itself on my window. I actually found it mesmerising. The tree's branches moving and dancing their silhouettes over my window really helped me to sleep as I lay on my bed, on my side, staring. There was always one shadow in the bottom left of the window, which I had assumed was cast from something more permanent outside. The corner of a roof for example, but to my mind's eye it had half a face, with the nose to one side and wore a flattened bowler hat. I thought nothing of it.

I don't remember what I did the weekend before we started learning about World War One, but I remember being excited at breakfast on the Monday morning. I wasn't enamoured with school, but I couldn't wait to get there that morning. I wolfed down my breakfast, grabbed my satchel and coat and with the usual farewell from mum and the instruction, "Don't dawdle!" my brother and I set off.

In those days, it was normal for kids to walk to school and we had to walk a mile across a communal green area to get there.

When we arrived, Steven peeled off to his class (he is one year younger than me) and I attended mine. Our teacher, Mrs Douglas, called out the names of our class pupils for registration to which we replied, "Yes miss." And then the lesson started.

We had an hour talking about how our British Army soldiers fought the German Army in the trenches and the senseless futility of fighting over scraps of land. As the lesson unfolded, I found myself sitting wide eyed in awe at the conditions and bravery of soldiers on both sides. They were truly horrific and there was no way any of us could comprehend how bad things were. Mrs Douglas was very careful presenting her class and we saw cartoons in books she had given us to depict what the soldiers wore and how they lived. We saw the odd old photograph of smiling British soldiers, disguising the horror of it all.

The rest of the day was spent doing the usual lessons of Arithmetic and English and other activities. At play time, the boys played War whilst the girls huddled together and took turns singing and clapping hands with each other.

That night, Steven and I returned home, had tea and before we knew it, we were in our pyjamas and sent to our beds. We always slept well. Not only did the shadows on the window aid me, but we did a lot of physical activity in those days.

Chapter Two: The introduction

I knew I was drifting into sleep as I watched the shadows of the branches swaying softly on the window. I felt my eyelids getting very heavy and as much as I tried to keep my eyes open to enjoy the spectacle, I slipped into a deep sleep.

"Adrian…" a soft Yorkshire accented voice called out at a low volume.

I kept my eyes shut; my body instantly filled with fear and adrenaline. I couldn't figure out if it was just a voice in my head, if my parents were talking about us and I heard my name, or a noise outside that I had mistaken.

"Adrian. Hello lad," the voice called out again.

"It's ok," he softly said, "I'm over here. Look at the window."

I was lying on my right side as usual and I trusted my instincts and opened my eyes. The voice sounded so friendly, so gentle and curiosity got the better of me.

I looked at the window and saw nothing out of the ordinary, at first. The permanent shape I had seen as a face, turned slowly towards me. I recognised the shape now. After having a lesson on British soldiers in World War One, the bowler hat now made the form of a helmet. The nose of the face was cast in shadow, but I knew he was looking at me. My heart was racing, I could hardly breath but I suppressed the urge to scream. I was totally confused and I was now wide awake.

"Who....who are you?" I whispered to him.

"I'm Humphrey. I've been waiting a long time to meet you," his gentle voice claimed.

"Are you.....a ghost?" I remember asking.

For some reason, I could tell Humphrey was smiling. His cheeks puffed out and his chin took on the shape that meant he was doing exactly that.

"Sort of lad. Does it matter? I'm here now. Are you scared?" he asked reassuringly.

I nodded small nods, "Yeah. I don't know. I think so."

He laughed a little, "I wouldn't expect you to be anything less. Don't worry."

"How long have you been waiting, Humphrey?" I whispered.

"Oh a long time young 'un, a long time. I've been watching over you, making sure you're ok and I've been waiting to introduce myself."

I smiled. There was something so gentle about the face, even though it was cast in shadow and also something so protecting.
"Are you a soldier?" I enquired.
"Yes. You're learning about soldiers in World War One aren't you?"
"Yes. Mrs Douglas started on it today."
"Well Adrian, I was in that war."
I was lost for words. I knew that, before me was the ghost of someone long gone. I didn't know whether to feel sad, happy or overwhelmingly privileged.
"Adrian, I'm going to go now. I know this is a lot to take in," he whispered.
"I'm going to come back though, is that alright?"
I nodded furiously, "Yes, yes. Please do!"
"That's great, goodnight Adrian."
"Goodnight Humphrey," I replied somewhat sheepishly.
The face turned to one side and moulded back into the permanent shadow I had grown used to. I lay and stared at it for a while and quietly called out to him again.
"Humphrey?"
After a few seconds of pause, I whispered out to him again but the shape didn't change. I knew I had to remain patient and returned to closing my eyes and falling to sleep.

The following morning, at the breakfast table, I didn't mention what had happened in the night. I think I started to believe that it had all been a dream. Whatever had happened, I couldn't wait to get back to school again to learn more about, what was called, the Great War.

My mother must have noticed something wrong with me though as I was being quieter than usual. As I stirred the milk in my Rice Krispies, I hadn't realised that I hadn't even eaten a spoonful.

"You alright Adrian?" she asked.

"Yeah fine. Sorry I was just thinking about something."

"Right, well, finish your breakfast and get off to school. And don't...!"

"Dawdle!" I finished the sentence for her. She smiled and I started to act normal and ate my breakfast.

I grabbed my coat and satchel, made sure Steven had done the same and the two of us said our goodbyes as we headed off to school.

Mum grabbed hold of me just as I was going out of the door.

"Hang on a second..." she said.

"Look at your hair, it's all sticking up!"

She proceeded to carry out my childhood pet hate! She licked her fingers and ran it through the parts of my hair that were sticking up, trying her best to flatten it and make sure her eldest child was presentable. "Right, off you go."

I grimaced in disgust and headed off for school, again.

Mrs Douglas called out registration and we all duly replied to signify our presence and I couldn't wait to get started on World War One again.

The lesson started with another book; this time it showed black and white photographs of soldiers in trenches. The clothes looked dishevelled and muddy, yet they all had the appearance of getting on with things.

We listened to Mrs Douglas as she talked about the trench systems that were dug by the soldiers and how there were three lines of trenches in parallel with each other. There was the front line trench, which was where all the assaults were started, the support trench behind that one and a reserve trench behind that. In between all the trenches, reaching towards the brigade headquarters were all the communication trenches. We learnt that this was where all the orders came from and they were delivered often by soldiers who were tasked to run between the trenches. It wasn't a surprise to learn they were called "Runners".

I didn't want the lesson to end and I groaned my disappointment out loud when the school bell rang to tell us all it was the end of that lesson. Mrs Douglas ushered us all out to the playground and my school friends congregated outside, with our pockets filled with marbles. Surrounding the concrete playground, there were lawned areas and we had scooped out shallow bowl-like depressions into the ground which the caretaker never touched. We started to play and at a suitable point I asked my mates, "Do you believe in ghosts?"

Tomo, the classes' tall boy, became quite animated. His eyes bulged in recognition of the question and his mouth opened wide.

"Yeah too right!" he said, excited.

"Me too!" came another excited reply from Simon opposite me, just as he was about to flick a marble.

All of a sudden, the marbles were ignored and I started to hear about all the ghosts my classmates had seen or heard about. I heard about the Drummer Boy of a local castle who had fallen asleep on his watch and the castle was attacked. His ghost inhabits the castle to this day, forever remorseful that he lost his life because he fell asleep. I heard about a Spitfire pilot who roamed the local woods, approaching people and asking for directions before disappearing right in front of them. I subsequently heard, later in life, about a Spitfire being excavated right in the very woods my mates were talking about.

I was surprised and delighted that my question was met with so much enthusiasm and it only made me more determined to keep the contact with Humphrey. I didn't utter a word about him to my classmates and the reason I asked the question was never brought up. I became more and more excited.

The day passed in a blur and Steven and I made our way back home. All the while I was almost wishing for nightfall so that I could don my pyjamas and go to my room. Mum greeted us from the kitchen with the usual pleasantry and dad was sitting in the living room, polishing his boots and watching television. I always enjoyed the smell of boot polish. It was one of those "love it or hate it" type of smells; a bit like petrol. At the dining table when we were eating our evening meal, mum asked us how our day at school went. I began to tell my parents about our lessons on the Great War and how our soldiers lived in the trenches. Dad took on a particular interest, being a soldier himself and elaborated a little more on the information I had from school.

"Has Mrs Douglas mentioned the artillery bombardments the soldiers used to suffer?" Mum interjected quietly, "He's too young to know about that yet," and dad smiled at her.

"Suppose so. It weren't nice in those trenches," dad continued in his own Yorkshire accent.

"My grandad was a soldier and when I were a kid, I remember asking him about what he did in the Army. He just used to say, "I were in t'Somme," and never said anything else."

We finished our evening meal and all sat in the living room to watch a bit of television. I think in those days, our bed time was about nine o'clock and at that asserted time, we were duly instructed to put on our pyjamas and hit the hay.

As usual, we changed into pyjamas, cleaned our teeth and mum said her goodnights to us both. I settled back in bed, rolled onto my right side and watched the shadows on the window.

The tree branches swayed slowly in a gentle breeze outside; side to side, side to side. As much as I fought the sleep to try and stay awake to hopefully talk to Humphrey, I couldn't keep my eyes open.

"Adrian....."

My eyes shot open with an adrenaline rush and I raised my head to look at the window. Humphrey's face was back again.

"Hello lad," he said so softly.

"Hello Humphrey. I've been learning more about the Great War at school!" I whispered, excitedly.

"Oh good! Are you enjoying it?"

"Yes. You were all very brave."

Humphrey hesitated a little.

"I could teach you more if you like?"

"Yeah that would be brilliant!" I leaned forwards slightly, accentuating my keenness.

"Well....I'll make this easier for us both. Can I come in and sit next to you?"

I couldn't believe this surreal experience that was only going to get better. For a fleeting second, I was apprehensive having gotten used to only seeing his face in silhouette.

"Yes, please do!"

The face faded and right before my very eyes, as I looked towards the wall opposite, Humphrey appeared before me in his uniform. I could see him from head to foot and the hairs on my arms stood on end.

He looked so smart. He wore his regimental hat with its badge, his wool coat and trousers, a wide canvas belt around his waist and what looked like a long bandage wrapped around the bottom half of each of his legs, from the top of each boot. I asked about them.

"What's those?" I asked, pointing at his calves.

He moved forwards and sat, crossing his legs.

"They're called puttees. They're meant to give us protection from the rain and mud, but they're pretty useless. If you wrap them tight enough though, they give you a sense of support on your legs," he laughed softly.

I looked at his face, which was still in darkness, but I could see his features a lot clearer. I could also see how young he was.

"How old are you Humphrey?"

He shifted his weight a little before answering, "I'm twenty eight. But to be honest there were a ton of my mates who were younger than me to fight in the war."

"Dad mentioned something about artillery that you all had to suffer. What's that?"

"Oh that. Yes. Well, that was something that both sides had to contend with. You remember your lesson the other day where you learned about the trenches?"

"Yes...."

"Artillery is basically cannon fire. Like in the really old days, ships used cannons to fire big balls of iron at each other to try and sink each other's ships. The cannons in World War One fired bombs which were aimed at the trenches."

It began to sink in why mum thought I was too young to learn about it. But she was wrong, I wanted to know more. I wanted to understand.

"Where's your rifle?"

"All in good time, young 'un. Have you got many lessons left then?"

"We have two more, then that's it. Mrs Douglas says we can learn more about it all when we go to big school; when we're older."

"Ah good. Are you enjoying school? Have you got many friends?"

"School is alright," I replied, shrugging my shoulders, "My classmates are alright too. The boys are enjoying the lessons, but the girls aren't."

Humphrey laughed, sitting upright a bit more as he did.

"That's only natural. Eventually they'll all learn to understand."

I was getting more and more curious.

"Did you hate the Germans?" I asked sheepishly, not knowing how he would react.

"Well.....some of us did. But most of us just saw them as other people. If they shot one of our mates, we wanted to shoot back, but it wasn't hatred. You'll laugh at this, but sometimes we used to whistle a tune and because their trenches were quite close to ours, they used to whistle with us!"
I could see him smiling at the memory and it was such a warm smile.
"We had our orders you see and so did they."
I thought about it for a couple of seconds.
"Mrs Douglas says that sometimes you were fighting over small areas of land and that in between the front trenches you called it "No Man's Land", is that true?"
"Oh yes. It was called that because the land belonged to no-one. After all those bombs it was full of craters, mud, barbed wire and all sorts of stuff. We had our orders to advance through it sometimes, but the Germans held us back quite a bit. Something Mrs Douglas might not teach you, but on the odd occasion we would all stop shooting at each other. Some of the Germans spoke English and we shouted across to each other, promising not to shoot so that we could meet up in the middle of No Man's Land."
I couldn't believe my ears!
"Gosh! What did you do?"

"We met in the middle, shook hands and swapped cigarettes. We showed each other photographs of our loved ones back at home and tried to learn about each other. After a while, we shook hands again, wished each other good luck and returned to our trenches."

"That sounds so sad!" I exclaimed.

"It was, kid. It was. But the war had to go on until someone surrendered."

We both paused, taking the time for me to sink it all in and also time for him to contend with the memory.

Humphrey sighed.

"Adrian I'm going to go back now, ok?"

"You'll be back though?" I asked, knowing he would be but also showing I wanted him to come back.

"Oh yes, definitely. You sleep tight now and I'll see you soon."

He stood upright, pulled his thick wool jacket down to straighten it, smiled and gave me a salute as he slowly disappeared.

I looked towards the window, seeing the still shape of his face and whispered to him.

"Goodnight Humphrey, goodnight," as my eyes quickly felt very heavy and I returned to my deep slumber.

Chapter Three: School lessons

School the following day, was attended after the usual breakfast, motherly instructions regarding how fast we were to travel and the flattening of hair.

After registration, Mrs Douglas continued her lesson on World War One.

This time she talked about how the British Army was the only army in the war which was volunteer, professional soldiers. All of the other countries used conscripts, which were men of the right age and ability who were instructed by their government to carry out military service. They could then be called up at the outbreak of hostilities. Britain didn't have enough men in its regular army though, so they appealed to their citizens to "Join Up" to their local regiment. In particular, a Lord Derby came up with the idea that local men could join up together and fight together in what became known as "Pals Battalions". It started off in London, but was more synonymous with the northern areas of England. She went on to tell us that the idea was never repeated, because when these men went into action a lot of them were killed. This created a huge gap in local communities and there was talk of a "generation wiped out" because of the loss of all those men.

Again I found the lesson absolutely captivating and I was dying to tell her what I knew from Humphrey. But I had to keep that as a secret and felt even more privileged that I had him in my life. For the time being anyway.

The rest of the day passed very quickly again. I lost my best marble during play time, but managed to cry it back again and there was no further talk about ghosts.

Back home we had our usual evening meal and dad wanted to know more about our history lesson.

"Learn anything else about World War One then Adrian?"

"Yep, we learned about the Pals Battalions today."

"Ah yes, the Pals. That was a big thing where I'm from in Yorkshire. We don't have them any more."

"Mrs Douglas talked about a generation of men being wiped out and it wasn't good for the local villages."

"Hmmm, it's well known. It was a good idea at the time because the local lads all wanted to be together, but it turned out to be tragic."

I was kicking my legs which were dangling from the dining chair whilst I thought about a question.

"Do you wear puttees, dad?"

"No son, they're not part of the uniform anymore. Where did you learn about them?"

"I just saw them in a photograph and asked Mrs Douglas about them," I lied to him.

He chuckled a little, "We still wear the hob nailed boots they used to wear, but they're mainly for parades."

I found it all fascinating but kept my secret. At the predetermined time, Steven and I went to bed with pyjamas on and teeth scrubbed clean.

As I lay in bed, on my side, staring at the shapes of the tree branches and Humphrey's face profile, I drifted into a deep sleep without hearing from him.

The following morning, I didn't give it much thought that he hadn't made contact as I knew he would be back. He said he would be back, so I had no reason to doubt him.

We got to school and I was saddened to hear that the day's lesson on World War One would be the last lesson. Mrs Douglas had a quick talk about the guns the soldiers used and how the soldiers were supposed to keep them clean all the time, despite the conditions. She talked about how the men used to sleep in dug out parts of the trenches, how poor the food was and how their clothes were treated for lice. They used a lit candle to run the seams over the flame, burning them off! When they were resting behind the lines, they had baths while their uniforms were boiled to get rid of them. The conditions sounded absolutely filthy, but there was always a certain humour about it all amongst the soldiers. Practical jokes were to the fore and they really made the most of their Rest and Recuperation (R and R) after their stint at the front line. It was interesting to me that the same regiment didn't spend long periods of time on the front line. In fact, the troops were rotated so that they spent less than a week at the front. She also taught us that when the soldiers were resting, they would also grab a fired brass artillery shell or bullets and create art pieces that were known as "Trench Art". They used rudimentary tools and techniques, often using hammers and nails, to carve out different motifs or patterns on the side of shells. We saw pictures of some of the most stunning, poignant art pieces I had ever seen (and have yet to see better).

At the end of the class, Mrs Douglas asked for a show of hands from those who enjoyed learning about the Great War. My hand shot up, quickly followed by all of the boys. The girls too, all gradually put their hands up and I remember I felt like crying.

I actually had quite a lonely play time after the class and I was lost in my thoughts about Humphrey and what all his pals had to suffer day after day. I couldn't wait to talk to him again. We all promised Mrs Douglas that we would continue to remember all of the service men and women who make sacrifices for the country.

Going home after that school day was a sombre experience as I dragged my feet through the grass across the communal area. I was particularly quiet during our family evening meal.

Dad must have noticed as we all sat around the table.

"Well Adrian? How was the lesson today?" he asked, blowing gently over his spoon of soup.

"Very good as usual dad, but it was the last lesson today."

"Oh? Why so sad then?"

"I don't feel as though I've learned enough about it all."

Mum laughed a little, "Don't worry about that at the moment. You've got the rest of your life in front of you; you'll learn more later."

I didn't reply, I just stirred my potato soup slowly.

Dad continued, "You know, Mrs Douglas can only teach you so much about that war. It was grim son, very grim and you're a bit young to know the gorey stuff," he quipped.

"I understood that when I asked my grandad about it all and he never wanted to talk about it."

I nodded and continued.

That evening, I went to bed at the usual time after carrying out my dental duties and lay on my side, in bed, watching the shadows dancing across my window again.

It wasn't long before I heard the familiar soft, low Yorkshire accent.

"Evening Adrian," the face looked at me again.

"Humphrey!" I whispered with excitement. "Come in, come in!" I preempted his question.

He laughed a little, "Ok lad, hang on."

I watched in amazement again as he appeared right in front of me as I looked at the wall opposite. He still wore his uniform, his features partly illuminated by the street light outside.

He sat in front of me, crossing his legs and leaned forwards.

"So how was school today?"

"It was ok, but I'm really sad."

"Oh? Why's that?"

"We had our last lesson on the war today, but I was telling dad earlier, I want to learn more."

Humphrey sat back a little, "Did your dad say anything else?"

"He said it was very grim and that Mrs Douglas could only tell me so much. I know I'm only ten, but I know I can handle it."

Humphrey bowed his head, but kept my eye contact.

"Your dad is very wise Adrian. Don't forget he's a soldier too. He's been to Aden and Northern Ireland so he knows what conflict is like."

"Yeah.....I suppose so."

I paused for a few seconds, "But I still think there's more we could have learnt!" I exclaimed.

Humphrey sat back a bit more, paused for a couple of seconds and leaned towards me again, fixing his elbows to his knees.

"You know, if you really want to know, I mean REALLY want to know, I can take you there."

My heart filled with excitement and felt like it wanted to thump its way out of my ribcage. I could tell my face was also flushing red.

I rasped out my whispered reply, "YES! Please Humphrey, I would really love that!"

"Hmmmm...." He thought hard about it.

"Ok then, but if I tell you to look away, cover your ears or both, you'd better do it! Ok?"

I nodded furiously, "Yes, yes!"

"Ok then..."

He stood up and straightened himself.

"Out of bed then, take my hand and close your eyes. I'll let you know when you can open them. I'll never let you go so don't worry."

I slowly and quietly slipped my legs from under the blankets and stood in front of Humphrey.

He smiled at me and held out his right hand. I have to be honest, I paused a little out of fear. I didn't know what was going to happen next, but I raised my hand and took his......

Chapter Four: Humphrey's journey

His hand felt rough, like a low grit sandpaper, but felt incredibly warm and strong. To his word, he didn't let me go as the sensation I felt was like flying without moving a muscle. I kept my eyes firmly shut and there was no sound, I just felt my entire stomach rise to my throat for a few seconds. I was so excited, yet very nervous at the same time. I still felt the warmth I could feel from my bedroom and Humphrey eventually spoke.

"Ok Adrian, you can open your eyes now."

I gradually opened my eyes, fearful of what I would see and the light of the day came streaming into my vision.

Before me I saw a rudimentary training camp, with soldiers marching around in formations, others in physical training clothes and lots of shouting from instructors! There were big, teepee looking, white tents all in a row in the background with soldiers all bustling between them. It was such a hive of activity and I took it all in as we stood there, hand in hand.

Humphrey looked down at me, smiling. I could see his features in the clear light of day now. He looked so young and handsome. So friendly.

"How are you feeling?"

I looked up at him, grinning from ear to ear. "Great! Where are we? Am I a ghost now?"

He laughed, "No! You've come back in time with me, so this is hard to explain. Our worlds are linked so long as you hold my hand. I can take you to the places in my memory, but nowhere else. You're safe, don't worry. Do you want me to tell you what's happening here?"

I looked around me, trying to soak it all in. "Yes please. Is this training?"

"Spot on. When we all signed up for the Army, we were all civilians from all walks of life. The Army had to discipline us, make us fighting fit and train us to obey orders no matter what. So we learned about trench construction, how to clean our kit and weapons, keep ourselves clean and everything military from the different ranks to how much we were going to get paid. The Army looked after everything."

I heard gunfire way in the distance.

"Is that the shooting range?"

"Yep. Want to have a look?"

"Too right!"

"Typical boy! Alright, hang on, close your eyes."

A sudden feeling of rushing for a second, waved over me as we whizzed our way over.

"Ok lad, open your peepers."

I opened my eyes to see a row of soldiers, lying on the grassy ground with their rifles, shooting at large squares of cardboard about one hundred yards away. Their instructors were walking up and down the line and making corrections to their rifles or the way they were shooting them. We stood to one side and I watched in awe. Not a single soldier looked in our direction and I could tell I was in a completely different realm of time.

"Were you a good shot Humphrey?"

"I was indeed Adrian. We were encouraged to shoot in miniature ranges where we used small bullets against very small targets. One night, for a bet, I put a penny up and shot it straight through the middle at twenty five yards."

"Wow! That's a small target!"

He smiled widely and said, matter of factly, "Won a bit of money that night."

We watched the soldiers shooting for a minute, then Humphrey looked down at me. "Do you want to see what happened after training?"

"Yes, great, this is amazing!"

"Well our battalion set off from here and we were transported to France by ship landing there in September 1915, so I'll take you over to France. Ready?"

I nodded quickly and closed my eyes, "Ready."

The rushing feeling enveloped me again. I felt like I was losing my balance a little, but I realised it was only a sensation.

"Ok, open your eyes."

If I thought the training camp was a hive of activity, nothing could have prepared me for what I saw next.

The French harbour was teeming with ships and men in uniform all disembarking from troop carriers, with cranes unloading large boxes of ammunition and supplies. The men walked off the ships by long gangplanks and I could hear their superiors shouting at them, barking a never ending stream of orders. Some of them looked very pale and I couldn't work out if they were nervous or suffered from sea sickness. The smell of the place was a mixture of seawater, thick smoke, diesel and weirdly, gun oil. It seemed to hang in the air, no matter how hard the wind blew.

We stood amongst it all, to the side against the wall of a harbour building and nobody batted an eyelid at us. I took in all the different cap badges from the soldiers. As much as their rifles, kit and clothing seemed the same, the regimental badges showed the difference.

It was busier than a bee hive and I held Humphrey's hand tightly.

"Ready for the front then?"

I slowly raised my eyes to Humphrey, "You mean the front line trenches?"

He slowly nodded, his face devoid of a smile this time.

I looked back at the scene before me and knew I needed to see how all this activity ended up on the front.

"Yeah. I'm ready."

Humphrey squatted so his eyes were level with mine.

I really noticed the detail in them; they were dark grey but so friendly.

"Now listen. If and when I tell you to close your eyes, you do that. I won't let go of your hand, but if I need to cover your ears, I'll do that so don't fight it. Ok then?"

I took a deep breath and held it for a couple of seconds, then exhaled when I had made my decision.

"Yep. Ok, let's fly."

Fly we did, or at least the sensation of it and before I opened my eyes when the sensation

stopped, I could tell we were somewhere
very different. Very different indeed.

"Before you open your eyes Adrian, I've
taken you to the Battle of Albert in 1918.
Now, we've already taken part in many
battles before this one, but I'm skipping
them to show you this one. Is that ok?"

Keeping my eyes closed and his hand held
tight, I couldn't hear or sense anything but I
replied, "Yes, that's fine Humphrey. Thank
you!"

"Ok then. As you open your eyes, do it
slowly so that your senses slowly open too
and take in everything around you. Try not
to be scared, ok?"

"Ok...."

Slowly I opened my eyes to see we were
standing on the top of the front line
trenches, that stretched away from me in its
familiar staggered, zigzag line. It was
actually a beautiful day. The sun was
shining, the blue sky was dotted with
dappled clouds and there was a gentle
breeze on our backs. Soldiers were all along
the lines. Some were in small groups,
smoking cigarettes and talking softly to each
other, some were reading letters from home,
some were writing home. Some of the
soldiers were cleaning their rifles and some
of them were fast asleep in shelves dug into

the sides of the trench walls. Then I watched as some soldiers appeared with hot food for the rest and there were cries of joy mixed with complaints, which were light hearted but also carried a message.

"Here comes slops!" I heard one of the soldiers cry out and Humphrey giggled.

"That's my mate Mersom!" he pointed.

I could vaguely see him, but I could see he looked like a jovial chap as he smiled at the soldiers carrying the food, with his rounded, ruddy cheeked face.

"They're having a laugh at least," I said to Humphrey.

"Oh you have to Adrian. There's enough misery going on. Take a look to your right, towards the German trenches."

I turned my head to the right and where I could see order amongst the trenches, No Man's Land was exactly the opposite. There were craters of different depths everywhere, some filled to the brim with water.

Shattered tree trunks littered the area and clumps of grass and weeds grew in small patches, surrounded almost completely by the mud. There was barbed wire and the detritus of war everywhere. Bits of uniform, shattered helmets, bullets and dead horses also scattered across the land as far as my eye could see.

I shook my head in disbelief, "Why would anyone want this?"

"Incredible isn't it? This is what both sides are fighting for; the very ground we are standing on. But this is only a small cog in a very large machine and unfortunately it's the men in these trenches who are all part of that machine and have to bear the brunt."

Through everything I could see and take in, one sound dominated and I searched the skies to find it.

Humphrey could see I was looking and he smiled and said nothing.

It was a bird singing and the sound was wonderful. Eventually I found it and the bird was so small, yet it seemed to flap its wings and not even move forwards.

"Can you see it then?" Humphrey asked.

"Yeah! Is that a Skylark? I learned about them at school."

"That's it! Lovely sound isn't it? In between all the gunfire, it's one of my favourite sounds. I love them."

I looked at Humphrey and could see he was smiling at the bird as it sang and flew its happy song. Humphrey closed his eyes and I could see he was lost in his thoughts, his face soaking in the sun. How I would have loved to have known what he was thinking about. Was it home? His family? Yorkshire?

England? Who knew, but I left him to it for a while. The sun was shining off his face and he looked really happy.

As I left him to his thoughts, I looked closer at the British soldiers and focused on one of them who was stirring from his sleep on one of the dug out shelves. He had his helmet covering his eyes, but as he woke and removed it, then placed his feet on the ground, turning more towards me, I instantly recognised him.

My eyes widened as the realisation dawned and I squeezed Humphrey's hand harder. Pointing at the soldier, I called out.

"Humphrey! Look!"

I looked up at him, my arm still stretched out as my finger pointed at the soldier. Humphrey followed my finger, then smiled in acknowledgement.

"It's you!"

"Yep. That's me alright."

But he didn't seem happy at all and seemed more to be shrugging it off than anything else.

We watched for a while as his living soul trudged down the lines, stumbling and carefully making his way to a larger dug out. Smiling at his chums and swapping quick jokes with them.

"That's me heading to see our OC. That's
"Officer Commanding", right before....."
Humphrey then bowed his head and looked
at his boots. He sniffed, shifted his weight
between his feet then looked at me.
"Adrian...." he said, a serious but worried
look on his face.
"Yes Humphrey?" I was getting confused
now.
"You've got to promise me something. I
need you to do something and you've got to
promise to do it."
"Yes, sure. It's the least I can do."
Humphrey looked at the landscape in front
of us and I could see he was fighting his
emotion.
He looked at me again and squatted in front
of me, "You've got to tell our story lad.
Sometime in the years to come, you've got to
tell our story. Don't let people forget what
we've done, will you? Please? Otherwise,
what have we done this for?"
I could tell we were coming to the end but I
didn't know what would happen next.
I answered without thinking.
"Yes, of course Humphrey. I won't let them
forget, I promise."
He pulled me towards him, tears filling his
eyes and he gave me such a hug. I could feel
the warmth from his body as much as I

could feel his emotion, but I couldn't shrug off the feeling that he knew something was going to happen.

"You've got to go now," he said as he gently released the hug and stood upright.

"What?! Why?" I asked, more out of being upset but fearing I would never see him again.

"This is where my journey ends Adrian and I can't allow you to see it. You can't. Close your eyes now, please, close your eyes."

"But will I see you again?" I asked in panic. I looked up at him and saw him fighting his tears, his chest heaving as he looked towards the sky.

As we stood and held hands, I closed my eyes and felt him slowly releasing his grip. I really wanted to fight it and keep hold, but I knew this was going to be harder for him as it would be for me. The Skylark had stopped singing its glorious song.

Just as he was finally letting me go, I heard him whispering.

"Never forget us, never forget us...." as his voice trailed off, it was replaced by the moaning of artillery shells as they announced their arrival, raining down on the trenches we had been looking at. At the moment they landed, I felt the very earth beneath me shudder and tremble at their impacts. For a brief second, I could feel the terror.

Chapter Five: Return to France

I never forgot about Humphrey as I made my own journey through life and I've done many different things since I was that ten year old boy.

Granted I didn't do well at school, but my upbringing meant I had lived with different cultures, learnt manners, learnt to be humble, learnt to be patient and understanding as well as the difference between right and wrong. Mum and dad did well.

There were strange but fitting coincidences as I have travelled through life, that have direct links to my brief time with Humphrey. Was he still watching over me? When I was old enough, I joined my local Air Training Corps (Air Cadets) and went gliding at RAF Scampton. Weirdly, the weather was always bright and sunny and when I rested in my uniform, lying on my back in between the duties and flying, I always heard a Skylark singing.

I got into shooting, mainly thanks to dad who bought us an air rifle at about the same age I joined the Air Cadets. I joined a local shooting club in 2007 and in 2010 we were having a shooting practice at one hundred metres. For a laugh, I taped a penny to my target board and took a shot at it. To my amazement, the penny disappeared signifying that I had hit it. I fully expected never to find the coin, expecting it to have flown into the distance. When the shooting stopped and we collected our targets, I felt something land on my right foot. I bent down to inspect what it was and to my disbelief it was the coin. Shot straight through the middle.

Dad finished with the Royal Military Police after a glittering fourteen year career. At first, he found work as a security guard for the Cash In Transit operations of Group 4 Security. But then he went to start a career with the Prison Service as a Prison Officer and he seemed to slip into the role nicely. We moved into our Prison Service house at the Ranby Prison, the estate being right next to the prison and we had a good group of friends.

Now, Dad was always passionate about gardening and we spent many an evening watching Gardener's World on television with the late, great, Percy Thrower and dad seemed to know all the latin names of any flowers that Percy showcased. I have to admit, his passion didn't transfer to his two sons, although I grow a few flowers in pots in my back garden.

Dad's real passion though, was (and still is) fuschias which he still grows today. When he was a Prison Officer, he had a little cottage industry, shall I say it, growing these flowers and either giving them or selling them away. His colleagues also asked for cuttings from his flowers, so good were they. Mum and dad eventually retired. They settled, as have their sons, in Northern Ireland. To some, a strange choice, but I've always said this little country is Europe's best kept secret. It has its political faults, but that's not for this story.

What I didn't know was that dad had started to trace the Hirst family tree and had found that there was a strong military history to the family.

I used to visit them regularly and as we sat in the living room of their house in Portrush, sometime in the year 2010, he said he had found the name of my great granduncle who had fought and died in World War One.

"Oh very good! What was his name?" I remember asking.

"Humphrey. Humphrey Hirst. He were a Private in the King's Own Yorkshire Light

Infantry. KOYLI's they call them. He's buried in France in the city of Rouen at the Saint Sever Cemetery. We're planning on going over to see him and then spend some time with your aunt and uncle in the South of France if you fancy it?"

On hearing the name my heart jumped! After all this time, some thirty two years later, I realised Humphrey was actually related to me. He didn't tell me that at the time, but it resonated with me as to what he meant about learning more in the years to come. Not only was he saying I would learn more about the Great War, but I would also find out more about him! To be fair, I could have asked him what his surname was at the time, but at ten years old I was too excited and naive to ask.

I didn't hesitate in accepting dad's invite and so the planning started. There's not much I like about this digital age we are in, but the internet was a big help in booking ferries and accommodation for the trip. To be honest, it was cheap enough. We (mother, father and I) were going over on our motorbikes with my parents taking their huge one litre engine BMW armchair on two wheels and me on my little boxer engined BMW bike too.

And so in August of 2011, we rode down to Rosslare Harbour and caught the overnight ferry to Cherbourg, France. It was a lovely crossing; a very calm sea and as we stood at the back of the ship, sailing away from Ireland, I got a sense of what Humphrey and his pals felt as they left Blighty.

The circumstances were obviously entirely different, but the feeling of heading off to foreign soil was there.

Credit where credit is due, dad had rigged his bike to his SatNav which communicated directions through headphones installed in his helmet and I followed.

We stopped at one point to take in a coffee and a bun and he explained a couple of wrong turns to me, quietly.

"Sorry about those odd turns there son, but I've got the SatNav giving me constant instructions and your mum gabbling on our intercom too!"

It dawned on me pretty quickly and I felt a bit of compassion for the fella.

We stopped in a small village which had been liberated by the Allies in World War Two, called Sainte-Mere-Eglise. The church in the village centre has a dummy dressed in an American soldier's uniform attached to a parachute that is caught on the church spire. There's a true story of an American

Paratrooper whose parachute got caught on the spire and he was left dangling down the side of the church. He was eventually caught by the Germans after he pretended to be dead for a while.

We travelled on to our hotel in Rouen, with plans to visit Humphrey the next day. Dad had worked out (as usual) that the cemetery was within walking distance of the hotel and so it was that we set off the following morning.

At the entrance to the cemetery, we were greeted by a lovely old French lady who asked if we needed any help.

My French is fairly good, so I asked her where the British soldiers were buried and if there was a flower shop nearby?

She told us the plots were at the rear of the cemetery but the flower shops were closed. It didn't matter much, dad had brought a small wreath of poppies and I had brought a small crucifix with poppy. As we walked through the large cemetery, the sun was blazing down and it was a wonderful day. We eventually arrived at the British section, depicted splendidly by the shallow domed headstones, immaculate greenery and shrubs at the foot of the stones. I really didn't realise how big the cemetery was as there seemed to be thousands of headstones. The experience of walking in these cemeteries is surreal. It's like the dead are thanking you for visiting them as their headstones look at you, all in formation, standing proud.

Dad knew the plot number of Humphrey's burial and so the search started.

We actually split up as we searched and I defy anyone not to feel any kind of emotion as you read the details of these brave boys. I saw their ages at the time of their death and a lot of them were so young!

Humphrey wasn't lying when he told me his mates were sometimes a lot younger than him.

Eventually dad cried out to us, "Here he is! I've found him!" and I walked towards him as he stood looking at the headstone. He was probably about one hundred yards away as I started my stroll to him and when I was close to him, my heart absolutely skipped. Of all the headstones we had walked by, of all the plants and shrubs that adorned them, when I got to Humphrey's, his was the only one to be surrounded by a fuschia bush! It was unbelievable and I had to turn away briefly to fight back the tears.

I imagined Humphrey smiling at us all and mouthing the words, "Thank you. You've found me."

If you don't believe anything in this book, please believe that the fuschia bush was there. It was such a spiritual moment and to this day I am lost for words.

Chapter Six: Present day

On Remembrance Day every year, I cry. I cry so hard at the memory of Humphrey, but also for the sacrifice his kind and all the subsequent service personnel have given. For the very freedom of me being able to write this story.

All wars are terrible, futile interjections in the history of mankind and yet we hear about them almost every day.

Of everything Humphrey taught me, I wish the world's leaders could also learn.

We are on a tiny planet, in a tiny galaxy in a huge expanse of a universe and yet we just want to kill each other.

Is there a God? Is there a supreme being? Have they abandoned us? I can't answer that, no one can, but I sure expect that Humphrey is looking on and is being looked after....until we meet again.

43084 Private Humphrey Hirst.
King's Own Yorkshire Light Infantry.

My penny!

The End.